ALPACAS DON`T GET ANGRY!

TAMMY FORTUNE
(THE AUTHOR)

A Special Thanks

To my family, for love and no drama!

Illustrator & Editor - Joanna Jarc Robinson, Ph.D.

Photographs © 2021 Mariah Fortune Photography

Butterfly Hill Farm – Home of Apollo and many other adorable alpacas. www.butterflyhill.net

APOLLO
(THE ALPACA)

Apollo the alpaca enjoyed the sunny day.
He galloped and he sprinted, he loved to play that way...
Then Lucy Llama leapt in, she wanted to play too!
But she forgot her manners, like llamas sometimes do.

Well, Lucy bumped Apollo and he got pushed aside!
She did not even notice! He felt so hurt inside.
Apollo could not believe what Lucy had just done!
So he mumbled to himself, **SHE RUINED ALL MY FUN!**

As he thought some more he scowled, **HOW COULD SHE BE SO RUDE?**
SHE NEVER SAID I'M SORRY. SHE SPOILED MY GOOD MOOD!
His hurt turned into anger and he started steaming.
Apollo didn't do it, but he sure *felt* like screaming.

Billy Bug crawled by and asked, "Hey! What is wrong with you?"
Apollo said, **I'M ANGRY. I DON'T KNOW WHAT TO DO.**
"Alpacas don't get angry," said Billy from down low.
"It's no big deal. You'll be fine. Why not just let it go?"

Apollo's **ANGER** doubled, and he wanted to spit!
Billy Bug was way off base – he just did not get it.
Apollo shooed him away then raised his voice and said,
GET LOST! YOU AREN'T HELPING! BUG SOMEONE ELSE INSTEAD!

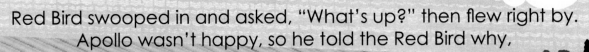

Red Bird swooped in and asked, "What's up?" then flew right by.
Apollo wasn't happy, so he told the Red Bird why,
I'M ANGRY! yelled Apollo, **IN FACT, I'M SUPER MAD!!**
WHAT THAT LLAMA DID TO ME WAS AWFUL — JUST PLAIN BAD!

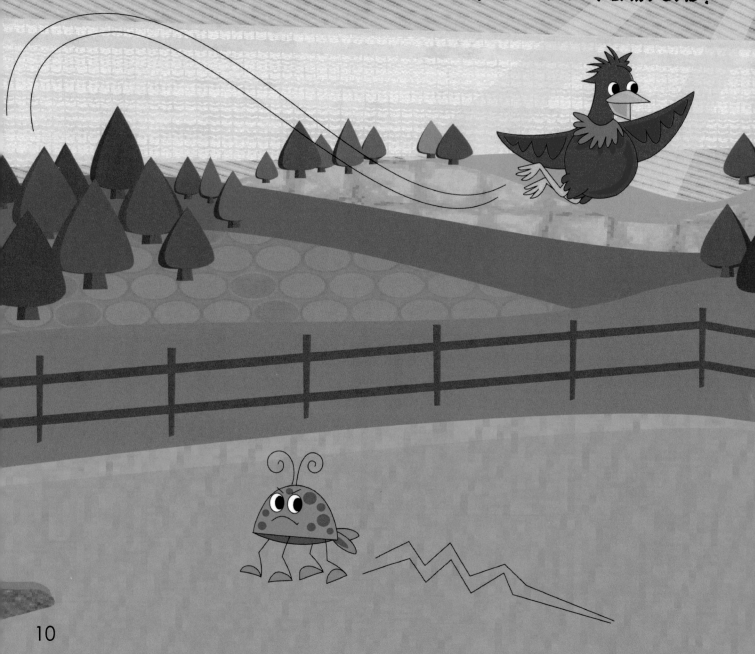

"Alpacas don't get angry," whistled the big red bird.
But then it flew off quickly, without another word.
Apollo felt MORE annoyed, and still, a little hurt.
He stomped his feet and snorted, while kicking up the dirt.

Now, to make things even worse, Ben Bunny asked him too,
"Hello, my friend, Apollo, what's going on with you?"
I'M ANGRY! screamed Apollo. I FEEL LIKE I COULD BURST!
WHAT LUCY DID TO ME WAS THE MEANEST - CRUELEST - WORST!

"Alpacas don't get angry," the small brown bunny teased.
Apollo glared at Ben. It's clear he *wasn't* pleased!
UGH! YOU DON'T GET IT EITHER! I DON'T THINK IT'S FUNNY!
Apollo's voice was SO loud it scared away the bunny.

13

Next a bumblebee buzzed in, as if things weren't bad enough.
And before Bert Bee could ask, he was greeted with a huff.
Apollo yelled, **I'M ANGRY! BUZZ OFF! LEAVE ME ALONE!**
But Bert would not give up and just circled like a drone.

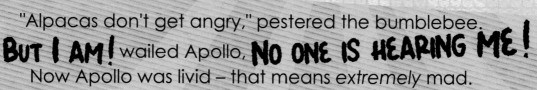

"Alpacas don't get angry," pestered the bumblebee.
BUT I AM! wailed Apollo, **NO ONE IS HEARING ME!**
Now Apollo was livid – that means *extremely* mad.
He felt like punching, kicking – or doing something bad.

Well, the farmer heard noises, like snorts and wails and such.
He had seen Apollo mad - but never quite *this* much.
The farmer asked him why and then listened with great care.
He didn't judge Apollo, he wanted to be fair.

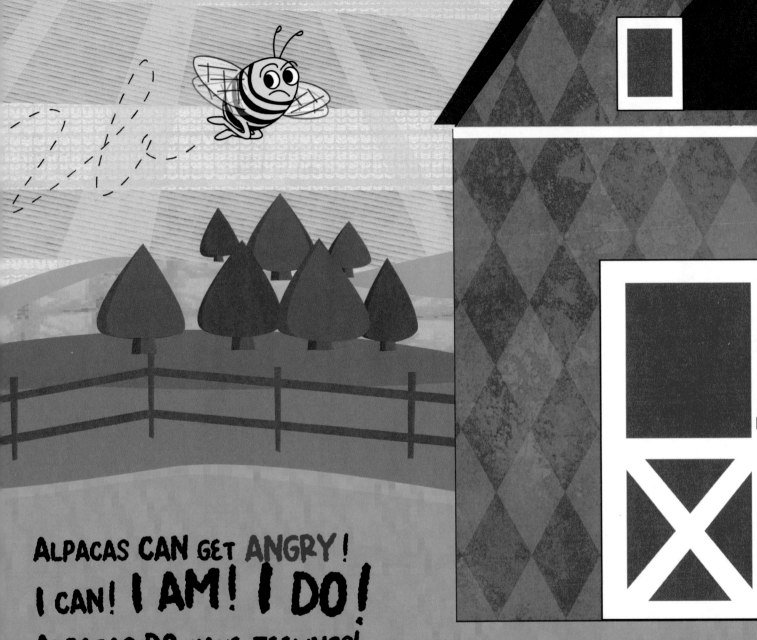

ALPACAS CAN GET ANGRY!
I CAN! I AM! I DO!

ALPACAS DO HAVE FEELINGS!
ALL CREATURES DO! IT'S TRUE!
ALPACAS CAN GET UPSET, OR WORRIED, PROUD OR SAD,
OR ANY OTHER FEELING — LIKE FRUSTRATED OR GLAD.

"You are right," said Farmer Joe, "I'm glad you kept your head."
You **can** express your anger – in safer ways instead.
Whenever I feel angry, I have a trick I do.
I focus on my breathing – and you can do it, too!

18

1

"First, you take a deep breath in,
slow and steady is best.

2

Then slowly let the air out...

3

...and take a little rest.

Keep on taking breaths until
you feel relaxed and chill.
I bet that trick will help you,
in fact, I KNOW it will!

So, Apollo filled his lungs, just like a big balloon.
And when he blew the air out, it felt like a

MONSOON!

Apollo soon felt better, his body had calmed down,
But yet for some strange reason, his face still showed a frown.

The farmer had an inkling about why this was so,
"If someone hurt your feelings, it's good to let her know...

Now that you have calmed yourself, it's easier to say,
'I felt really angry when you pushed me in that way.'

Apollo went to Lucy and asked her for a chat.
He said, I FELT ANGRY WHEN YOU BUMPED INTO ME LIKE THAT.
ALPACAS DO GET ANGRY. I WANTED YOU TO KNOW,
I TOOK DEEP BREATHS AND TOLD YOU... NOW I CAN LET IT GO.

24

"I'm **so** sorry I hurt you," replied Lucy Llama,
"I really did not mean to cause you so much drama.
Can we please be friends again? I'd really like to play.
We should be having fun on this bright and sunny day!"

Apollo forgave Lucy and off they went to play.
Luckily his angry mood did not destroy the day.
ALPACAS CAN GET ANGRY! Who knew? It's true! They do!
Apollo also calmed down - and you can do that too!

The End

Don't BEE sad...

**If you liked (or loved) Alpacas Don't Get Angry!,
check out these other books by Tammy Fortune:**

Did You Say Pasghetti? Dusty and Danny Tackle Dyslexia

Dusty's Big Oops

You can find out more about Tammy Fortune
at www.TammysTeachingTools.com

You can find out more about Joanna Jarc Robinson
at https://jart1473.wixsite.com/joannarobinson

Mama says...

Nobody is better than you and you are no better than anybody.

www.jkmhappy.com

ISBN 978-0-9820686-8-7

T2-ERA-731